BY LEA TADDONIO ILLUSTRATED BY ALESSIA TRUNFIO

LUCKY 8

#2 The Curse of Deadwood Hill

MIDDLE SCHOOL

Spellbound

An Imprint of Magic Wagon
abdopublishing.com

To Jarah, Bronte and Poppy — LT

To my Family, my Love, my best friends and Eva. Thank you all
for helping me to make it real in all your personal ways. — AT

abdopublishing.com

Published by Magic Wagon, a division of ABDO, PO Box 398166,
Minneapolis, Minnesota 55439. Copyright © 2018 by Abdo Consulting
Group, Inc. International copyrights reserved in all countries. No
part of this book may be reproduced in any form without written
permission from the publisher. Spellbound™ is a trademark and logo
of Magic Wagon.

Printed in the United States of America, North Mankato, Minnesota.
092017
012018

Written by Lea Taddonio
Illustrated by Alessia Trunfio
Edited by Heidi M.D. Elston
Art Directed by Laura Mitchell

Publisher's Cataloging-in-Publication Data

Names: Taddonio, Lea, author. | Trunfio, Alessia, illustrator.
Title: The curse of Deadwood Hill / by Lea Taddonio; illustrated by Alessia Trunfio.
Description: Minneapolis, Minnesota : Magic Wagon, 2018. | Series: Lucky 8; Book 2
Summary: On their first day at their new school, Makayla and Liam learn their house is cursed
    After some research, the twins learn a girl - Jo Ann George - who once lived in their house
    disappeared. Does the Magic 8 Ball have something to do with her disappearance?
Identifiers: LCCN 2017946549 | ISBN 9781532130540 (lib.bdg.) | ISBN 9781532131141 (ebook) |
    ISBN 9781532131448 (Read-to-me ebook)
Subjects: LCSH: Blessing and cursing—Fiction—Juvenile fiction. | Ghosts—Juvenile fiction. |
    Elementary school environment—Juvenile fiction. | Brothers and sisters—Juvenile fiction.
Classification: DDC [FIC]—dc23
LC record available at https://lccn.loc.gov/2017946549

TABLE OF CONTENTS

CHAPTER 1

Doomed

Mom pulls up in front of our new school. It looks like something straight from a movie.

"Time to meet my ," I mutter in a deep voice.

I see Mom's eyes roll in the rearview mirror. She thinks I'm being a *drama queen*.

6

"Thanks for the ride." My twin

brother, Liam, opens the door.

"Look on the BRIGHT side, Sis.

You aren't the only new kid today. I'll

be right beside you while everyone

stares."

I glance around the school yard

as we walk toward the front door.

"Um. Liam? Everyone really is **staring**. *And* whispering."

"Yeah." Liam's smile faDes.

"*And* pointing too."

"What class do you have first?"
I'm suddenly **AWARE** that I'm
going to miss him. I've never been the
new kid before.

He tugs a **SCHEDULE** from his
back pocket. "History."

9

"I have gym. Ugh." The idea of

PLAYING volleyball or basketball

with total strangers makes my stomach

hurt. I'd rather do art or theater class.

The bell **RINGS**.

"See you at lunch." Liam runs  the stairs.

As I walk toward the gym, three girls start talking behind me.

"That's her all right!" one whispers. "With the long, black hair."

"Her family bought Deadwood Hill?" another asks. "You couldn't pay me a **MILLION** dollars to set foot in that place."

14

"Think she knows what happened last year?" a third girl questions. "With the witch's CURSE?"

A chill runs down my spine. What curse? Are they talking about the Deadwood Witch? Maybe we really are DOOMED.

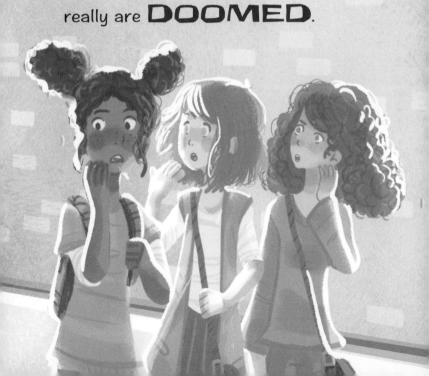

When I reach the locker room, my heart is **POUNDING**. I love watching HORROR movies. But I don't want to live in one.

My thoughts turn toward the Magic 8 Ball. That strange toy makes me NERVOUS. But I could ask it about the CURSE.

CHAPTER 2

Witching Hour

I eat lunch with Liam. We sit at the end of a long table. People are still **LOOKING** in our direction.

"Hey, take a picture, it'll last longer," I *SNAP* at a curly-haired boy who keeps staring. He turns around while his friends laugh.

19

"How is that whole making new friends thing working out for you?" Liam bites into his peanut butter and MARSHMALLOW sandwich, his personal favorite.

"I don't have time for friends." I bite into my own sandwich. "We have bigger **PROBLEMS**." I fill him in on the CURSE.

"Let's ask the Magic 8 Ball." Liam pushes his glasses 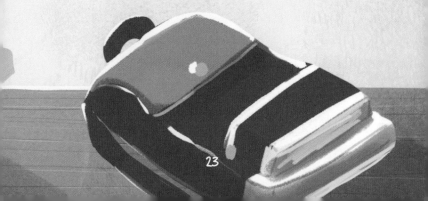 his nose. "It will tell us the truth."

"It's not great that a magical toy isn't the creepiest thing about our new house." I take a GRIM sip of chocolate milk.

At the end of the day, we ride the school bus home. As we walk up the long driveway to our house, worry sets in.

Maybe it isn't a smart plan to talk to the Magic 8 Ball. Especially when we don't know who is talking back.

Liam unlocks the front door and *RUNS* straight to the Magic 8 Ball on the shelf. There is a loud *CRACK* of thunder when he picks it up.

esn't move. He keeps

ATING those two words.

hour. Witching hour."

a **DEEP** breath and grab

8 Ball from his grasp.

." He bends over and grabs

. "What just happened?"

coughing.

That can't be good. The sun

is **SHINING** outside. Not a

CLOUD in the sky.

Liam's **EYES** roll back in his head. "Witching hour. Witching hour," he **MOANS** in a strange voice.

He do

REPE

"Witching

I take

the Magi

"Who

his knees

he asks,

"Let go

run away, bu

He might be

my brother.

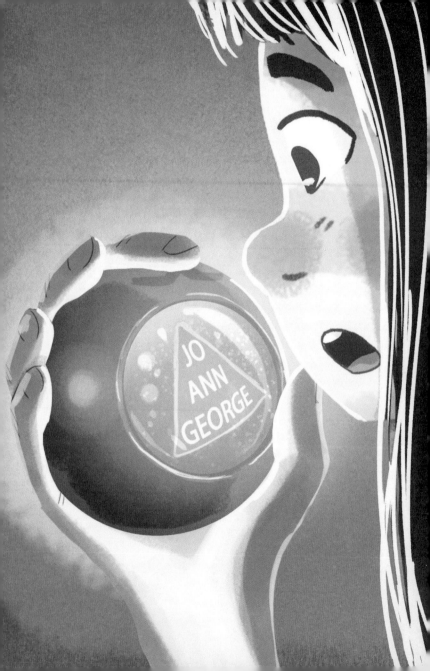

I can't answer. Not when my mouth is DRIER than a desert.

The little TRIANGLE behind the Magic 8 Ball's window spells out the words: *Jo Ann George*.

Who the heck are Jo, Ann, and George? Are they part of the Deadwood Hill CURSE?

CHAPTER 3

Jo Ann George

Liam and I stay away from the Magic 8 Ball for the night. We don't tell Mom and Dad. We'll figure this out A L O N E.

The next day at school, Liam and I spend lunch in the library. Again, kids *stare*. We hear whispers like, "Deadwood," "the CURSE," and "new in town."

Liam is PALE and has DARK circles under his eyes. He can't remember what happened when he touched the Magic 8 Ball. But he hasn't eaten and looks like he saw a *ghost*.

I TYPE the words, Jo, Ann and

George into a library computer.

"Add Deadwood Hill and curse,"

Liam whispers.

The search engine loads a list of
newspaper articles. My heart DROPS.
"Are you seeing what I'm seeing?"
Liam *leans* forward in his chair.
The **HEADLINES** are scary.

"Jo Ann George?" I GASP.

"Those weren't three names in the Magic 8 Ball. It was one name."

"She lived in our house." Liam points at a picture on the screen. His hand shakes.

"Could October 30 be the witching hour?" Liam asks. He JUMPS up and trips on his chair. The Magic 8 Ball rolls out of his backpack.

Chapter 4

Help Me

"Are you CRAZY?" I hiss. "You brought that thing to school?"

"No!" Liam polishes his glasses. "I didn't put it in there. I swear."

I glance back to the computer and then back over to the Magic 8 Ball. "I'm sick of being AFRAID. I want answers."

When I pick up the Magic 8 Ball,

a ceiling light **BURSTS**.

A **fog** surrounds me.

I'm aware of Liam calling my name,
but he seems far, far away. The white
triangle is *spinning*.

"What do you want?" I whisper.

The triangle stops: *I want to come
home. Please help me.*

"Home?" I ask. "Where is home?"

Deadwood Hill. The triangle *spins* again and stops. *I am Jo Ann George. Help me, please.*

When I **BLINK** again, I'm laying on the floor.

"What happened?" I **rub** my head. It's tender and sore.

"You **SCREAMED** and fainted." Liam looks worried.

I stand **UP**. "Do you have the Magic 8 Ball?"

SCHOOL LIBRARY JOURNA

He holds up his backpack. "In here."

"We have to go. Now." I run for the

EXIT.

"Where are we going?" Liam

CHASES after me.

"Back home. We have to find a way

to help Jo Ann George."